ABOUT THE BANK STREET READY-TO-READ SERIES

More than seventy-five years of educational research, innovative teaching, and quality publishing have earned The Bank Street College of Education its reputation as America's most trusted name in early childhood education.

Because no two children are exactly alike in their development, the Bank Street Ready-to-Read series is written on three levels to accommodate the individual stages of reading readiness of children ages three through eight.

○ *Level 1:* GETTING READY TO READ (Pre-K–Grade 1)
Level 1 books are perfect for reading aloud with children who are getting ready to read or just starting to read words or phrases. These books feature large type, repetition, and simple sentences.

● *Level 2:* READING TOGETHER (Grades 1–3)
These books have slightly smaller type and longer sentences. They are ideal for children beginning to read by themselves who may need help.

○ *Level 3:* I CAN READ IT MYSELF (Grades 2–3)
These stories are just right for children who can read independently. They offer more complex and challenging stories and sentences.

All three levels of The Bank Street Ready-to-Read books make it easy to select the books most appropriate for your child's development and enable him or her to grow with the series step by step. The levels purposely overlap to reinforce skills and further encourage reading.

We feel that making reading fun is the single most important thing anyone can do to help children become good readers. We hope you will become part of Bank Street's long tradition of learning through sharing.

The Bank Street College of Education

To Byron to read to Karah
— J.O.

To Cara, Eliza, and Dana
— C.D.

Please visit our web site at: www.garethstevens.com
For a free color catalog describing Gareth Stevens Publishing's list
of high-quality books and multimedia programs, call 1-800-542-2595
or fax your request to (414) 332-3567.

Library of Congress Cataloging-in-Publication Data

Oppenheim, Joanne.
    "Uh-oh!" said the crow / by Joanne Oppenheim; illustrated by
Chris Demarest.
        p. cm. -- (Bank Street ready-to-read)
    Summary: On a dark and windy night, the animals in the barn
are frightened by strange noises on the roof and think that it might
be a ghost.
        ISBN 0-8368-1753-2 (lib. bdg.)
        [1. Domestic animals--Fiction. 2. Sound--Fiction.] I. Demarest,
Chris L., ill. II. Title. III. Series.
    PZ7.O616Uh   1997
    [E]--dc21   97-1629

This edition first published in 1997 by
Gareth Stevens Publishing
A World Almanac Education Group Company
330 West Olive Street, Suite 100
Milwaukee, Wisconsin 53212 USA

Printed in Mexico

3 4 5 6 7 8 9 06 05 04 03 02

"Uh·Oh!" Said the Crow

by Joanne Oppenheim
Illustrated by Chris Demarest

A Byron Preiss Book

Gareth Stevens Publishing
A WORLD ALMANAC EDUCATION GROUP COMPANY

WHOOOO!
It was a dark and windy night.
In the barn, all the animals
were sound asleep.

4

Just before dawn there was
a terrible THUD!
"Uh-oh!" cawed Crow.

"What was that?" mewed Cat.
"I don't know," cawed Crow.
"It's up there," whinnied Mare.
As she pointed to the loft,
there was another loud THUD!

"Uh-oh!" cawed Crow.
"What was that?" mewed Cat.
"It's up there," whinnied Mare.
"Sounds like spooks!" honked Goose.

8

Now the whistling wind
swept around the barn
calling WHOOO! WHOOOO!
And from the loft
came the frightening sound of
THUD!
        THUD!
                THUD!

"Uh-oh!" cawed Crow.

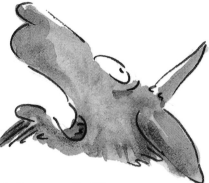

"Might be a ghost!" bleated Goat.

"Don't say that!" mewed Cat.

"It's up there," whinnied Mare.

"Must be spooks!" honked Goose.
"What bad luck!" quacked Duck.
"Go back to sleep," baaed Sheep.

But Crow, Goat, Cat, Mare,
Goose, and Duck
were too scared to sleep.
They sat side by side, shaking with fear.

"I know," cawed Crow.
"Someone has to go up in the loft
to see what's there."
"I'm afraid!" Donkey brayed.

Again the wind cried
WHOOO! WHOOOOO!
And a loud and terrible
THUD!
        THUD!
                THUD!
rumbled from above.

"What now?" mooed Cow.
"Might be a ghost!" bleated Goat.
"Don't say that!" mewed Cat.
"It's up there," whinnied Mare.

"Who will go?" cawed Crow.

"Nix! Nix!" peeped the Chicks.

"Sounds like spooks!"
honked Goose.

"Go back to sleep," baaed Sheep.

Crow tried to stay calm.
But now all the animals
in the barn
were wide awake and worrying.

Crow thought and thought.

Finally he had an idea.
"Let's draw straws.
The one who draws the longest
must go up to see what's there."

"Not my job!" grunted Hog.
"Nix! Nix!" peeped the Chicks.
"Not right now!" mooed Cow.
"No such luck," quacked Duck.
"I'm afraid!" Donkey brayed.

Again the wind howled
WHOO! WHOOO!
And something overhead went
THUD!
   THUD!
      THUMP!
"It's a ghost!" bleated Goat.
"It's up there," whinnied Mare.
"What bad luck!" quacked Duck.
"Sounds like spooks!" honked Goose.
"Don't say that!" mewed Cat.
"Go back to sleep," baaed Sheep.

"Uh-oh!" cawed Crow.
"I guess I know who has to go."

And saying that,
Crow gathered up his courage,
spread his wings,
and disappeared into the dark loft above.

Hog, Cow, Duck, Donkey, Goat, Mare,
Goose, Cat, Sheep, and the Chicks
sat as still as stones,
waiting and listening.

All at once there was a storm
of THUDS and THUMPS
and Crow began to caw,
"Uh-oh! Oh, no!"

And hearing Crow,
they all ran for the door—
mooing and grunting,
baaing and peeping,
mewing and braying,
honking and bleating.

And running outside,
they heard the thudding sound
as the wind hit the apples
that hit the barn
that hit the ground!

28

And up in the treetop
they saw brave Crow
jumping on the branches, cawing,
"WATCH OUT BELOW!"

"Some ghost," bleated Goat.
"So much for spooks!" honked Goose.
"Such a scare!" whinnied Mare.
"What good luck!" quacked Duck.
"I saved the show!" cawed Crow.

"Glad I stayed!" Donkey brayed.
"Let's eat!" baaed Sheep.
"I'm for that!" mewed Cat.
"Right now!" mooed Cow.
"That's my job!" grunted Hog.
"First picks!" peeped the Chicks.

So all that day and into the night
they munched and crunched apples
till the moon turned bright.
They munched and crunched apples
one by one,
they munched and crunched apples
until there were none.